CHEWING'S CHIKKI

CRUNCHY FOODS FOR THOUGHT

DEEPALI G.

First Edition: May 2021

Typeset in Comic Sans MS

ISBN: 978-81-951535-2-7

Cover Design: Debabrata Sahoo

STORYMIRROR
Stories that reflect you

Publisher: StoryMirror Infotech Pvt. Ltd.
                145, First Floor, Powai Plaza, Hiranandani Gardens, Powai,
                Mumbai - 400076, India

Web: https://storymirror.com
Facebook: https://facebook.com/storymirror
Twitter: https://twitter.com/story_mirror
Instagram: https://instagram.com/storymirror

Cheeselings and Chikki - crunchy foods for thought...

By Deepali G.

Magical meanderings and jovial jottings on Nature - life experiences for all folks young at heart.

This book is dedicated to all the cute and sweet children I have interacted with - who taught me & made me rich. Thanks to all the great managers, colleagues, teachers and friends I have interacted with, in all these years !!

Dedication

All my actions, thoughts and poems are dedicated to my favourite God.

Ganpati Bappa Moraya !

Table of Contents

S.no	Name of poem	Page no
1)	Filling Up My Dreams	9
2)	Here Comes The Rain !	12
3)	Dauntless warrior !	15
4)	Breezy Breeze	17
5)	Heavenly Grace !	19
6)	The divine chick	21
7)	Little Tears !	23
8)	O Elfie	25
9)	Perfect picture !	27
10)	Melody	28
11)	Variety is the plum policy !	29
12)	My mind	32
13)	Journey into Tinklesea	33
14)	Birdie Dear	36
15)	The divine voice	38
16)	Faith	40
17)	Solitude	42
18)	So Like Vegetables !	44
19)	Mango	47
20)	A Cartoon Dream In Verse	48
21)	Thought	52
22)	The Great Little Ant !	53

Hello young folks,

Nature is an infinite and unending fountain of constant Inspiration for all human beings ! A person who worships Nature and makes it a part of his Life, can never ever be disappointed and will always be rich. Creativity flowers with Nature. Poems are such miniature works of Art. Poems are perfect like cartoons and capture the essence of Life ! Do you know how I thought of this poem and others ? Well....I had quietly closed my eyes and very honestly was day-dreaming about the trees, flowers and birds around me. The flowers were gently falling from the trees on the road. They were of different colours & the entire scene was so picturesque that words could not express my feelings. I was in a really good mood to paint, but would paints really show my happiness ? But then I took my favourite pen and paper, began writing and the poem below got formed. You can too, want to give it a try? Who knows you also might dream and be a blooming, budding poet in the making ? This is one of my favourites....

1) Filling Up My Dreams

Many various colours

Dids't I in dreams see;

Borrowed them I, from

Nature's colourful moods

Many several varieties.

Stole some I,

from Beauteous flowers,

Mingled them, then

With Heaven's high showers,

But could fill them not

Even a little or in part,

Those, my li'l sweet dreams;

So empty like feathers

In the mind's heaven they fly;

Softly sail they away,

With tweeny li'l chirpings,

Whilst I, in a dreamy daze

Canst only blink wi' misty gaze.

They heeded me not,

And oblivious of me,

They glided past;

And though they are

My friends not,

Bids't them I, a

Teary goodbye.

*(One fine day…..Reclining lazily against a tree trunk, I was gazing at the delightful cluster of creamy white flowers overhead, when I saw a little green bird sitting on an electric wire. It had a pointed needle-like tail and its beak seemed sharp. The head was brownish in colour. As it nodded its head here and there, sideways a little fly happened to fly past in a teasing manner. The little birdie was trying to get at the insect, sitting on its aery perch. It moved its head furiously and snapped its beak every now & then. The fly would have been amusing itself, I'm sure. I walked down a little on the path, when a strange sound banged on the drum of my ears. At first I thought it was a bird calling but found out later that it was only a squirrel waltzing its way on the branch of a high tree. It was swishing and swooshing its fat furry tail. The feeling I had was simply great ! It seemed to me that I was in an enchanting place. A fairy place it seemed, or rather a fairy moment of time. Time stood still or rather, we can say that time sat still !! I wrote thus…)

> The feeling
>
> Like the moment,
>
> So magical be ;
>
> One would scarce
>
> Believe it true.
>
> The twig grew wings
>
> And then it flew !!

(The bird I saw was exactly the same colour as the twig on which it sat !!)

Here comes the rain

With a resounding clomp,

Walloping in the water

With swift-footed pomp.

Announcing itself as

An awaited visitor,

A business executive

With polite aplomb.

Hear the rain

Now cometh, in

Gentle slow descent,

Sounding like many

Merry little bells.

Hear the rain

Swishing fast,

Whistling unto itself

A timeless song !

A tireless craftsman

He is, the happy fella

Minting li'l chocolate coins

In the wet brown mud.

Coins that into the

Metal water melt.

Can folks not pay

In coins of chocolate ?

It seems to ask

Every human entrant

On the scene,

It seems to want

To take to task.

Ah ! the rain !

It's a busy tailor

For sure, weaving

Little water caps

For tiny li'l elves !

*(The rain means everything to us, doesn't it ? Rain means pure happiness, the most wonderful miracle of Nature ! When plump rain drops descend on the trees, plants, flowers and birds are in their best form. They are all decked up in royal finery that leaves you mesmerized. The divine presence is felt everywhere and we begin to believe that we must all be made of star stuff !)

Every time the rain gives us an entirely different experience isn't it ?

One such fine day, the promise of a sunny day was halfway to completion when it suddenly turned dark and cloudy & it started to rain gloriously. The scroll of the clouds unfolding slowly was a wonderful sight ! I went out and could feel the softness of a heap of chiffons in the little rain drops ! Rain was falling like thin satin ribbons that looked a lot like white vermicelli.

3) Dauntless warrior !

The velvet

Darkness of

The night,

Is with

Ideas

Bordered,

All over,

Like lace

With even

Exact space.

Like forms

On the cream

Of milk,

White enough,

But not

White still.

The mystery

Darkness of

The night,

A quiet

Impressive

Empress,

But also,

A cool

Dauntless

Warrior, who

Has no time

To fear.

*(You know something ? I had this habit of sitting up late for my studies in school. The atmosphere would be cool and the stars in their heaven, blinking oh so beautifully !! The moon would be there ofcourse, illuminating everything on the earth. I thought of this warrior poem & wrote it in one go ! I somehow felt then that creativity blossoms at night also. You get good ideas, you are at peace with yourself and the world, as it stops whirling around. Some of you will agree with this I am sure ! Something clicks inside and you feel like painting the whole world !!)

What is life

Without a little breeze ?

The one that whistles

Through the trees,

Or one that with

A person moves,

With him wherever

He happens to go.

Or one that in the

Mind doth arise.

It shakes a dozen

Sleepy thoughts.

Its speech serves

As two or more

Alarm clocks.

No one understands

How it comes,

An' wherefore it goes.

'Tis just a fairy tale

An' nothing more !

*(The importance of the wind in our lives cannot be underestimated. It makes us feel more alive and vibrant. The wind catches hold of us, and we are woken up from our deep slumbers. It spreads good cheer and we feel we should start dancing with the wind in the background. So penned a tiny po'm on the great wind....)

The wind blows its pipes

Like twenty trumpets

And violins nine.

Its celebration time

And the bells chime !

The children squeal,

As 'tis a grand meal.

5) Heavenly Grace !

Such is heaven's

Grace sometimes,

That thinking

Is found

Empty an' vain.

When one

Is only left

With wonder

An' scarcely

Anything more;

A strange

Baggage at

Your feet;

Can anyone then

Expect more ?

When Heaven

Sends showers

Of kindness

Down to Earth

Why do we

Stay snuggled

Up indoors ?

Why do we

Build roofs

On our heads

And not wait

For the sun

Instead ?

*(I think when happy thoughts merrily go round and round in the mind, then only we can understand that we have been blessed and realize the real value of our presence on the earth. We know then that these moments are golden and to be kept as prized possessions and used with pride. Isn't it ?)

Once I went to a beautiful garden with pretty pink roses & other flowers in various shades of pink and lavender. They all seemed to be dressed up smartly and sporting fresh green ties to match their pretty pink faces. On the wire fence, not very far away were some cherubic young of the sparrow family who seemed to be playing 'kho-kho'. Their quick movements looked so very funny.

I wouldn't so much

Have minded,

Had my dream

To an egg turned.

For then, if someone

Would fain like it broken

An' would then

Strike it hard;

Merely would I watch

It from afar.

I would shed not

So many tears, for

The li'l golden bits

An' would not go about

Helter-skelter, arm'd

With tape, paste or glue;

But would wait, and see
With a breath most bated
For a fuzzy golden thing
To peep from the wreck,
An' thank sweet Heaven
For a gift most divine !!

*(I suppose if this could be turned into a cartoon, then it would be more great ! For that is how it emerged in my mind, as a sort of picture of what I felt. Somehow one has this dissatisfaction that words do not really capture your feelings and emotions. But we cherish these words nevertheless, because they serve as reminders of your emotions at that point of time. These poems are like paintings and photographs which capture those frosty moments and are frozen works of art which give limitless joy. They are compressed, packed and tied with coloured ribbons. The person who receives this ornamental piece has to untie it, encase it in a flowery frame and hang on the wall for timeless inspiration !!)

*(Sometime at night one day, I happened to see a lovely insect on the white wall of the kitchen. It was pale green and seemed to be wearing a lace gown that fitted it well !! I felt like saying to it...)

You are so pretty,
And so tiny,
And so small,
And you know nothing
Of the world at all !!

22... *Cheeselings and Chikki*

7) Little Tears !

When the cover of cloud
Over mine eyes, turns
Dark, dreary and dull,
For a moment or so
It seems to lull.

But then, it
Storms and rages,
And begins to pull apart
And punch, the mind's
Nifty neat recesses.

A pool of water an' salt,
Then collects in each eye,
They flow as li'l oval tears
That to the ground plop.
And lo ! have they become
Little opal creatures.

In eagerness for life,
They flit about softly,
Drunk are they from
The spring of Life,
They bubble and chuckle.

But as I paused
To look at them,
With magnifying eyes,
In utter fascination,
They too vanished
All in a jiffy,
Like the unhappy tears
In my eyes.

*(Once when I was sad, I scribbled the lines above on a lovely piece of coloured paper and then felt better. The sadness was transferred onto paper and I felt free of it ! On a similar note another small po'm goes as...)

There were seeds of sorrow
In the ae-er,
Floating oh so dully;
I bid them come not,
But into the soil of my mind
They'd stealthily crept,
Like unwelcome guests,
Like unwanted foes.

8) O Elfie

O Elfie ! Won't you sing a merry tune ?

A tune as sweet as ever can be

To proclaim God's reign on Earth ?

Tunes, sweet an' sour an' savoury,

Blissful, Heavenly and earthly ?

Tunes that make one feel as

If in the glowing heavens we lie,

Beside the sparkling vivaciousness

Of the gushing fountains high ?

O Elfie ! Won't you sing a joyful melody ?

That'll make one with excitement tingle ?

That'll make the stony silence still,

Or make flowers like bells jingle ?

O Elfie ! Please do do sing,

For it makes me sway an' swing,

O Elfie ! Do do da sing,

An' I promise to give

You a precious ring !

*(We all had been to a small village sometime during the rainy season, many years back. There seemed to be vibrations even in the grass. The water in the puddles seemed to reverberate noiselessly. The trees were making all sorts of dance poses. The clouds seemed to want to pick up the gigantic mountain boulders like a baby is picked up from its cradle. Saw a gorgeus blue jay and a coffee-brown birdie. Sculpted raindrops softly slunk and shimmered on the leaves. The trees were assuming all sorts of shapes. One of them looked like a horse and the one close to it like a woman trying to load the horse. As we rested under some trees, spotted a very strange worm. At first it looked like a stem as it showed no signs of being a living thing. It had such tiny feet that they were hardly noticeable. It had small pink circles over it, which we noticed on closer inspection. It was as still as a stone for quite some time. So we were about to throw it away, when it moved slightly and we jumped with excitement. Nature has given such a neat camouflaging to this little being ! It was a rather plump worm, certainly it could have been the fattest of its species ! Further down there was a lake and the birds we saw were a real treat for the eyes and ears ! So many birds had assembled at one single place ! The purple moorhen was the one I liked the best as it not only looked stunning but it made sounds like a flute ! I came back home and wrote this poem - O Elfie .....)

9) Perfect picture !

The radiant flowers,

The free butterflies,

Look a perfect picture

Of health and harmony.

In elegant synchrony,

With a flowing symphony.

Can anyone have

A better company ?

Away from the heat,

Away from the

Dust and noise,

Far from the breakless,

And the breathless

Madding city life !!

*(The other day I saw a sweet little white butterfly that gleamed whiter than any cloth washed with the best detergent ! It was daintily flitting about & creating patterns in the air with its amazing aery ballet dance !)

10) Melody

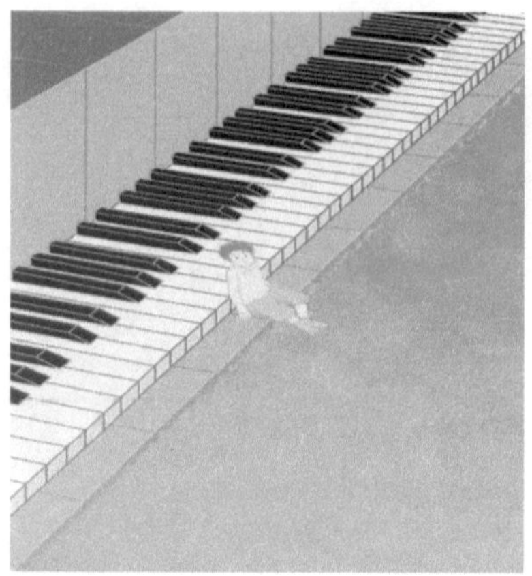

When a li'l

Soft melody

Tugs at your

Heart strings,

Like a li'l babe

Her mum's skirts,

The heart sings

In applause

An' in assertion.

It gives melody,

A Homeless

Lonesome wanderer,

A place in

It's guest-room.

*(Music is the best thing gifted to mankind ! We get so absorbed into it, that we forget ourselves and gain extraordinary insights and unlimited inspiration !)

11) Variety is the plum policy !

When Day One

Be the same

As Day Two,

Of what use

Would then be

These different days ?

When they bring

Not with them

Pleasantly nice surprises

Or youthful jollity

Or excitements

Least numbered one ?

If everything then

Be just the same

As the very next;

If butter would

Be the same

As bread,

And one story

Same as another.

Why then, there

Would be nothing

New to know.

If caterpillars would

Be the same

As fishes,

And butterflies

The same

As bumble bees,

Everyone will

Everything know

And everyone

Each other one.

Of what use

Then, would such

A life be ?

Where a person

Would like

A stone be.

For even one

Stone be not

The same as

Any other.

So Variety

Seems to be

The plum policy

Of beauteous,

Bountiful Nature !

*(Talking of God's creatures, just narrating my funny encounter with a creature that I saw some time back. I had been to my friend's place one day and was waiting for her in the parking area. There were some two wheelers & a car there. As I was waiting there & admiring the chikoo trees in the adjacent house & the greenery there, I was suddenly shaken from my reverie. I was sitting on the parked two-wheeler and my legs were above the ground on the foot-rest. A long mongoose with fiery eyes shook himself so violently as it saw me there and made such a frightening noise that I checked out my heartbeats later on, as they collided hopelessly into each other for a few minutes. Whew ! What a great relief ! Maybe it was angry with me that I sat there in its usual pathway. I heartily thanked God that my feet were not on the ground and there was a distance of three feet between me & the super-angry mongoose ! It left off in a huff & I continued admiring a white cat comfortably sitting on the stump of a tree)

12) My mind

My mind is then,

Sometimes still

Or sometimes movin'

Like a mill.

It will listen not,

And do what it will,

Even then I like it still,

As it flings down ideas

Like the puffed-up flowers

Softly falling off from trees.

*(The mind is such a vast, huge, enormously massive thing, isn't it ? We can stuff so many cluttered facts & bits of information & knowledge in it, and even then there is space for more ! I believe that my mind is like a chocolate box. So long as the chocolates are there it is sweet and fine. But when they get finished and get gobbled up in glee.. well then, they need to be filled up again !)

13) Journey into Tinklesea

When the wind is afire

With imagination,

It gently awakes

The sleepy waters,

The blue blinking waters.

It gently shakes

The winking leaves.

Lend me your eyes,

Your mind and your ears,

Says it to the

Lake and the leaves,

For I've got a

Song to sing for you

And a poem enclosed

In its covers too.

And so the wind

Sang for eternity,

Whilst the lake

And the leaves

Listened in harmony.

The lake grew

Deeper by this thinking

An' as it sat with

Swiftness drinking,

Sweet thoughts and

Wet honeyed words.

It drifted into sleep

And then, awhile

Dreaming silently,

Smiled unto itself

A toothless smile,

Like a li'l babe

Well-contented in sleep !

And so they say

In Tinklesea,

For many years now

When travellers chance

Upon the happy sight,

They surely see,

The wind deeply singing,

To the lake well-sleeping

And the leaves sweetly nodding,

In delight approving,

All in unison nodding

Like bright soldiers

In uniform performance.

And so ends the

Tale of the lake,

The wind an' the leaves

Of Tinklesea.

*(I once thought of the following fab cartoon idea ! A little girl gets transformed into a paper doll of white ! She slides down a slide of paper sheet, long and thin – winding away later to form a roll. The air is paper crisp and thin, as she sings a papery song. She swims in a sea of paper rolls which are white as snow. As she swims further, she joins another sea of paper rolls that are in various pastel shades. She feels exhilarated and enchanted and moves on further.... Sometime I plan to string my thoughts together like beads in a necklace and make a cartoon out of it.... It helps to be hopeful.. isn't it ?)

14) Birdie Dear

Where thou goest

Birdie dear ?

Cutting thro' the air

Like a knife thro' butter.

How thou melteth

In the air,

When thou art

Not snow ?

How then do thou

Mingleth, with the air ?

Were thou made of ether

Or born of some

Material better ?

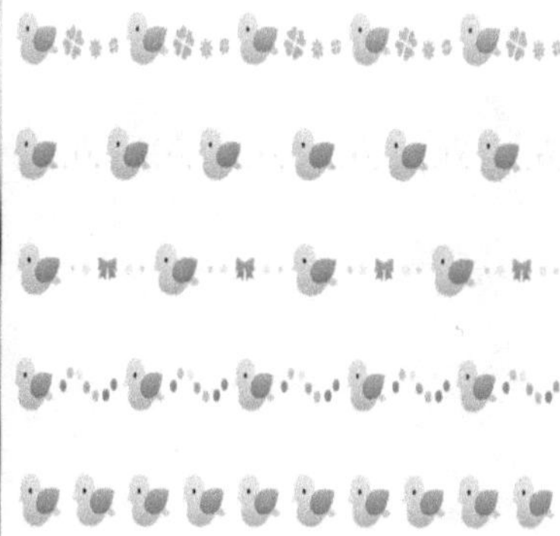

*(Looking at birds I sometimes feel a certain sadness ....Why? The reason is that unfortunately, the world's most stunning and dazzling creatures fly far too high in the sky ! But a million thanks are due to all those who take painstaking efforts to bring these extraordinary and overwhelmingly cute birds into our homes, through all those dedicated enthusiasts via our televisions, computers, mobiles and whatnot. These lovely dainty creatures make our life so colourful and musical. They are always there for us, like our best friends. They bring so much gladness and pure joy in our lives. The other day as I was walking on the bridge on a pleasant morning when I heard a quaintly attractive voice which said "quock", "quock." A queer-looking baby kingfisher was taking a bird's eye note of the goings-on above and below. It moved its head up and down as if uncomfortable of the neck which Nature had provided his head to rest on !

I am somehow very jealous of these feathered friends. They are not only a cut above the rest of God's own creatures but also smarter, stylish, dashing and so good-looking ! They do not do any exercise, work-out, weight-lifting or jogging but they are always fit as a fiddle and in the pink of health. They do not eat any exotic food or do any "riyaz" but their sound and song everytime is always tuneful and joyful ! Their look is the same everyday and yet they manage to surprise us with their youthfulness, vitality and sheer energy ! The best packages come small !!

The divine voice spoketh,

Through the language

Of the wind,

And the waterfall;

The cooing of the wind

And the chattering

Of the waterfall.

A voice that a

Muse happened to hear,

An' he like an angel,

Bright and pure,

Felt it echoing

Into his very heart,

An' this echo flowing,

Like a river

In motion, unceasing,

Unheeding, unmindful;

Ah ! 'Tis nothing

But, boundless

Ecstasy overflowing !

*(As we were taking a walk in the woods one day, saw so many wonderful things. A little ray of golden sunlight was travelling like a tram on a silken cobweb. It was heading back and forth with swiftness all the way ! There were some cobwebs beside the stream, between some bushes. They were so beautifully woven, that they looked like castles. They were sprinkled with dew drops which displayed all the splendid colours when the sun shown mildly upon them. After some time a dense fog got collected and acquired a reddish orange colour with a little yellow thrown in due to the lamplight under which it moved. It came with the breeze, moved in a rectangular column sideways towards a wall where we were standing. It came rushing, turned and twisted and then quickly made its exit. It almost seemed alive ! I kept having my fill of the scene as it was being replayed by the wind itself. The slopes looked festive with yellow and pink flowers. As we sat by the sparkling scenic stream, soaking in the scenery, the mist suddenly approached us and generously sprinkled us with dew. The place looked enchanting where we could expect to see humming angels and fairies emerging from the mist... amidst the bubbly silvery stream !)

16) Faith

If faith hath wings,

Then you will surely

Be able to fly.

In the chariot of fire

You may rise

And still remain

Unburnt, unscathed.

As separate as oil

From clear water.

If that be so,

The Past can

Be waved off,

The Present could

Be made a

Willing friend.

And the Future

Gazed at

With owlish eyes ?

*(What does living mean for me ? It sometimes means a lot and sometimes so little that I get surprised by the extremities. The swing from one to the other is funny. But more so living means faith, so we are tranquil and then take good decisions and do good work. Exploring Nature strengthens our faith. Scribbled these lines on one such day when we were out in the woods....)

Scarce have I known the woods,

And still I've loved them;

Like long-lost friends they seem to me,

Like affable dears they do greet me,

Like some warm host they do treat me.

Am I a departing traveller to them,

That they so lavish me with sweet treats ?

17) Solitude

Ah ! Sweet Solitude !

Teach me the talk

Of the whispering leaves,

Though tongue they

Have not and

Nor any ears,

But I think,

They hear me

Going past,

Like faithful

Pets they

Closer come,

Murmuring sweet

Nothings, an'

Moving away.

O Great Solitude !

Teach me to sing

Rambling songs,

That to the

Heart doth please.

Teach me to sing

Like the breezy wind

That comes an' goes,

An' yet, has peace,

Carrying a satchel

Of detachment

Packed an' full,

That it carries

With itself, an

Inseparable bundle

Clutched very tight,

An' won't let go

However anyone's might.

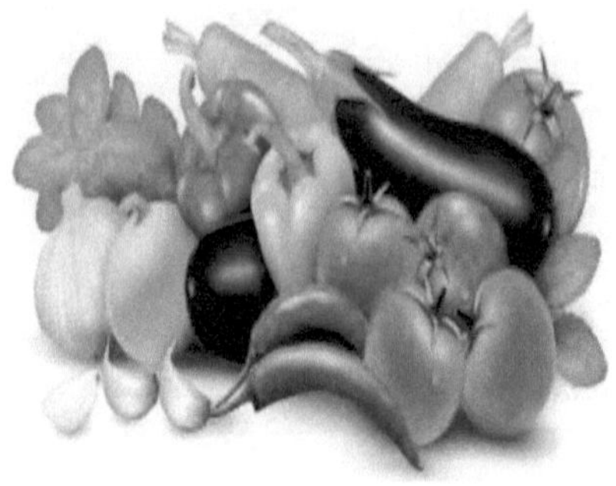

The wind is so like a cucumber,

Clean, cool, chill and tender.

The clouds are pure and snowy-white,

Like the inside of a pumpkin white.

The trees like giant cauliflowers stand,

Staring from their green aery height.

And all human beings ?

Oh, How I wonder !

Some like Ladies Fingers,

Cool, collected and elegant,

Some like little potatoes,

Stuffed and very haughty.

Some few like tomatoes,

Plump, sweet and loquacious,

Some like purple brinjals,

Always rude and grumpy.

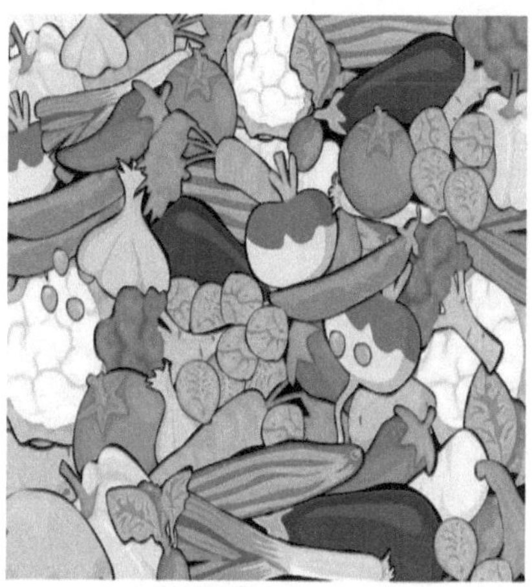

Some like dreamy peas,

Almost always naughty.

Some like sunny lemons,

Always fresh and healthy.

Some like the drumsticks,

Thin, Lean and grim.

Some like fresh mint,

Tangy and so greeny green !

And the little cabbage,

Calm, quiet and silent.

And what of French beans ?

They sit on mountain-tops,

Viewing all vegetables,

And the carrot is the best by far,

The genius of all vegetables !

*(As I hummed these words I was lost in thought... Some words remind us so much of food. When you say candidate, you are reminded of candy and date. The buttercup flower reminds you of butter in a cup. I heard some beautiful pink flowers are called ice-cream flowers...and scores of many many more....Can you think of some more ?

I thought of this vegetable po'm as a cartoon. And then the words were born and emerged gradually. The natural colours of vegetables are so amazing ! Each vegetable has its unique qualities and characteristic taste and smell.

The next mango poem was born on the sunlit terrace as I plunged into a mango. The king of fruits is doubtlessly everyone's favourite. We feel like kings and queens as we feast on this lip-smacking, juicy fruit. Our heart is full and the mind too when we explore the innumerable food combinations of this great, sweet and sour fruit.)

Sweet Heaven

Hast granted

A lovely boon

To mankind.

For in the

Mango is found,

Tastefully filled,

The gold of

The morning sun,

The sugary

Lusciousness

Of life and the

Happiness of the

Glorious Heavens !

20) A Cartoon Dream In Verse

Oh I wish

I'd be a fly

And fly along

With Time.

Ah ! to be

Fellow-fliers

That would

I dare

To happen.

For that

Certainly is,

My most

Fond dream.

 Yeah ! to

Fly faster

Than even

The Wind.

To teasingly fly

And run away

So, in rapturous

Glee, that even

The Wind would

With jealousy

Be jolted.

Ah to see !

It's green

Glaring glance.

Ah ! the

Very moment.

Oh ! the

Very time.

Ah ! to be

Able to say

To the wind,

Beware be

Thou sweet

Li'l chappie.

For here

I come.

Thou might

As well pack

Up and go

For a week-long vacation.

For you well-deserved it

Or so I heard,

But far too long

You've been Busy

busy Blowing things !!

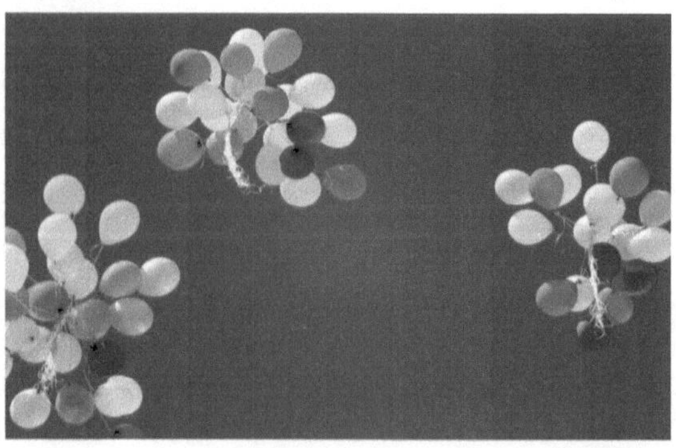

*(Talking about the wind ... caught a playful mood of the wind once.. the wind was giving itself a furious shake for as it was noiselessly shaking rain droplets dispersed in the air,they landed on my face. It seemed as if the wind had made a brush, dipped it into the rain water and sprinkled playfully over me.

Talking of cartoons, there are many situations in life when you feel like having a big laugh as some people or animals strike you as they behave like cartoons. While going in the bus one day, when the conductor rang the bell, a cat day-dreaming on the middle of the pavement woke up with a start ! A little later, when she was herself again the look on her face seemed to say, " Phew ! Mew ! It was that silly red container carrying those staring humans ! how silly of me to get frightened !" A nonchalant shake-up of the furry head was then followed up by a cool dignified catwalk, like a pompous white-robed monarch. The whole scene struck me as exceedingly hilarious ! I wish.. I could have made a small cartoon out of this. I think cartoons are the best of human creations. They strike a common chord with everyone and fill the lives of children with abundant happiness. When you are feeling low, a cartoon always enlivens everyone almost instantly like munching cheeselings and chikki ! Tried it ? So let's pep up and forget all about strange viruses like corona !!

Afterall, this life is a busy-busy business, so let's be like a buzzing busy bee !)

21) Thought

Wordless thought

With unease swims,

Like a lone babe

Unused to water.

Left it is all by itself

To splash about

Its hands and

Feet and reach

The nearest shore.

*(The inseparable blending of thought and words is simply amazing. Which comes first, you really begin to wonder ! It's a treat to watch a little baby expressing itself through its own language. It is such a huge effort to speak its first words.

Words makes the world go round and round. We cannot imagine a world without words and their subtle interplay. This intricate and colourful weaving of words makes our life so worthy. So we need to pick our words well to make the most nice effect. We pluck the best fruit from the tree to eat. Don't we ?)

22) The Great Little Ant !

How thou goest

Past the lump

Of delicious sweet,

White as the clouds,

Past such an

Exciting feast ?

How thou goest

Past, so oblivious

Of such a treat ?

Oh, great little ant !

Oh, how indeed ?

*(When in school, watching ants was one of my favourite past-times. Their constant movement always intrigued me. Their migration from one wall to another as also from one room to another and their prompt presence when anything sweet was kept anywhere in the house baffled me. Submerging them swiftly in water when they troubled me was what I liked immensely. (Surely, everyone likes this !) However, looking at them we can only say- Let's move on...Let's march on.......)